BEYOND
THE
ATTIC DOOR

TRACY DEL CAMPO

WESTBOW°
PRESS
A DIVISION OF THOMAS NELSON
& ZONDERVAN

Scriptures taken from the Holy Bible, New International Version®, NIV®.
Copyright © 1973, 1978, 1984, 2011 by Biblica, Inc.™ Used by permission of
Zondervan. All rights reserved worldwide. www.zondervan.com The "NIV"
and "New International Version" are trademarks registered in the United
States Patent and Trademark Office by Biblica, Inc.™ All rights reserved.

WestBow Press books may be ordered through booksellers or by contacting:

WestBow Press
A Division of Thomas Nelson & Zondervan
1663 Liberty Drive
Bloomington, IN 47403
www.westbowpress.com
1 (866) 928-1240

Because of the dynamic nature of the Internet, any web addresses or
links contained in this book may have changed since publication and
may no longer be valid. The views expressed in this work are solely those
of the author and do not necessarily reflect the views of the publisher,
and the publisher hereby disclaims any responsibility for them.

Any people depicted in stock imagery provided by Thinkstock are
models, and such images are being used for illustrative purposes only.
Certain stock imagery © Thinkstock.

ISBN: 978-1-4908-3707-9 (sc)
ISBN: 978-1-4908-3708-6 (e)

Library of Congress Control Number: 2014908572

Printed in the United States of America.

WestBow Press rev. date: 06/12/2014

Dedicated to my children,
Madison and Zion.

"The heavens declare the glory of God;

the skies proclaim the work of his hands."

—Psalm 19:1 (NIV)

Introduction

In 1859, Charles Darwin's *On the Origin of Species* was published. The "creation versus evolution" debate began, generating scientific and religious discussions around the world.

This argument came to a head in 1925 when John Scopes, a schoolteacher in Tennessee, was arrested for teaching evolution, creating a firestorm of tension between those on opposing sides of the fence. His subsequent trial, in July of that year, would be known as the "Trial of the Century" as well as the "Scopes Monkey Trial".

Beyond the Attic Door begins during this tumultuous time in history. Writing this book gave me the opportunity to weave together a few of my favorite things: history, humor, adventure, and, most importantly, faith.

Even though the "creation versus evolution" war continues to wage, new and exciting discoveries are made every day that reconcile science with the Bible. When we evaluate the evidence, it is quite clear that science confirms Scripture, which in turn confirms a wonderful and magnificent Creator.

Tracy Del Campo
January 2014

Chapter 1

June 1925

School is out for the summer, and eleven-year-old Lulu and her seven-year-old brother, Buddy, are on their way to visit their grandmother who lives in the forested hills of the Missouri countryside. Small farms, nestled in the valleys, dot a landscape that is surrounded by caves, bluffs, and hollows. It is a hot and humid evening when they arrive. The drive was long, nearly two hours from St. Louis in the back seat of the 1917 yellow touring sedan.

Lulu's honey-brown hair is in disarray, and her white dress is now covered in dust, due to the seemingly endless miles of gravel road. She tries to wipe the dirt from her freckled face, but eventually she gives up. She can hardly wait to run barefoot in the soft, thick grass; it's one of her favorite things to do. Her new, patent-leather shoes that her mother recently purchased at a fancy department store downtown will get a nice, long break while at her grandmother's. Except for Sundays, when she has to put them on again for church.

Buddy catches a glimpse of a wild turkey in the tall brush and quickly jumps out of the parked car. He lets out a loud Indian war whoop and heads off in hot pursuit. Jack and Otis, Buddy's faithful dogs, jump from the car as well and take off after their master.

Lulu can smell the distinct scent of a sweet-pea vine that winds up a trellis and leans against the white, clapboard house. She helped her grandmother plant it during her visit last summer.

The sun is beginning to set, casting a soft orange and pink glow across the horizon. Fireflies are flickering about in the fields and woods that surround her grandmother's home. She loves to catch the gentle bugs and put them in an old jar. At night, they twinkle like little stars in her room.

Crickets and frogs sing their usual harmonious chorus as they usher in the evening. The hustle and bustle of the city is long gone, and time seems to pass at a much slower pace.

Prone to daydreaming, Lulu often imagines that she is a fair maiden in the beautiful English countryside. She pretends the old, weather-beaten farmhouse is really a castle and some young, dashing prince will ride in on a white steed and whisk her far away. She's never told anyone about these romantic thoughts, except for her cat, Princess, who would never tell a soul. Thank goodness! She glances down at the gray and white cat on her lap. Princess looks around cautiously, unsure of her new surroundings.

"It's all right," Lulu says while stroking the cat. "We're at Grandma's house."

Bang! The screen door swings open, and her grandmother, Gertie, rushes out onto the porch.

"You're finally here!" she declares, wringing her hands with excitement. Lulu and Buddy's uncle, Hugh, a brilliant scientist and inventor, emerges from the house as well.

"Oh no, here comes trouble!" he announces with a grin on his face. His mother gives him an elbow to the ribs.

Lulu and Buddy's mother, Sybil, ascends the porch stairs and exchanges hugs with her mother and brother.

"Yes, we are finally here," she says with a sigh as she dabs her forehead with a handkerchief and takes off the cloche hat sitting atop her bobbed blonde hair.

Lulu runs and gives her grandmother and uncle a hug as she holds Princess in one arm.

"You've grown a bit, I see!" exclaims Gertie, who gives Lulu a kiss on the head.

"Yes, a whole two inches since Christmas," Lulu announces proudly. "Soon, I'll be as tall as you, Grandma."

"Where's your little brother?" Gertie asks, glancing toward the car.

"He's off chasing some critter," Lulu responds nonchalantly.

"Well, don't just stand there. Come on in," says Gertie as she opens the screen door. "You must be hungry."

"Wait for me!" says Warren, Lulu and Buddy's father, as he takes the suitcases from the car.

They enter the house and Warren sets the luggage down by the front door. He removes his cap and hangs it on the hall tree. Glancing in the mirror, he runs his fingers through his dark, wavy hair, adjusts his bow tie, and proceeds to the kitchen.

On the table is a glass pitcher of lemonade and a fresh cherry pie hot from the oven. Warren rubs his hands together and takes a seat at the dining table. "Cherry, my favorite!" he exclaims, eyeing the tasty treat before him.

"I've got a pot roast and potatoes and carrots as well," Gertie announces.

"Mmm," responds Lulu. "*My* favorite."

"Lulu, dear, can you get the plates?" her grandmother asks. Lulu goes to the hutch, counts out six plates, and places them on the well-worn wooden table.

"Go call your brother, please," says Sybil as she takes the silverware from the drawer.

Lulu opens the screen door and steps onto the porch. "Buddy, it's time to eat!" she yells at the top of her lungs.

"I'll be there in a minute," he responds from the dense thicket.

"Now!" Lulu insists.

"All right! You don't have to be so bossy, Sissy!" Buddy soon emerges with a few prickly burrs matted in his unkempt brown hair. He adjusts the round glasses precariously perched on his nose and wipes a bead of sweat running down his dirt-smudged face. "I almost had him," he says with a scowl. Disappointed, he climbs the stairs and brushes past Lulu.

"And don't forget to wash your hands," Lulu says over her shoulder.

"I know!" replies an exasperated Buddy.

Jack and Otis, exhausted from the hunt, lie down on the porch. Lulu gives the two dogs a pat on the head and goes back inside.

Hugh starts to pile food onto his plate. His mother, unhappy with his table manners, gives him a stern look and clears her throat.

"Warren, would you mind saying grace?" she asks, smiling at her son-in-law.

Warren nods his head, anxious to dig into the pie.

"Lord, we thank You for Your provision. We ask that You bless it. In Your name, amen."

"Amen," the others respond in unison.

Immediately, Warren reaches for a knife and starts to cut the pie.

"So what do you think about the Scopes trial coming up?" Hugh asks looking at Warren.

"Is that the man in trouble for teaching evolution?" Lulu interrupts.

"Yes, Mr. John Scopes," Warren says licking his fingers.

"It's the biggest news in the country right now," Hugh says in-between bites. "The trial starts next month."

"Yes, I know," Warren responds. "It's all over the headlines."

"What's the big deal?" Buddy mumbles with his mouth so full he can barely speak.

Sybil gives her son a disapproving look.

"It *is* a big deal," Hugh says, looking at his nephew. "People are questioning the authority of the Bible and the existence of God. The papers are saying that religion may be doomed," he says, shaking his head in disbelief.

A contemplative look comes over Lulu's face as she turns to her father.

"We didn't really come from monkeys, did we, Dad?"

"Absolutely not!" Gertie interjects.

"But I heard Mr. Peabody say that there is no God and Darwin is right."

"A fool, in his heart, says there is no God," Sybil adds, weighing in on the matter.

"Who is this Mr. Peabody, anyway?" Gertie asks, unable to hide her irritation.

"Our new neighbor," Sybil replies. "He sits on his porch all day, moaning and groaning about anything and everything to whoever will listen."

"For heaven's sake, Lulu, stop listening to him!" Gertie chides.

"What do *you* think, Uncle Hugh?" Lulu asks with obvious concern.

"Well," Hugh begins as he wipes his mouth with a napkin, "evolution is *not* a scientific fact; it's merely an assumption with no observational evidence. The important fossils that would support that theory have *never* been found."

He clears his throat and continues. "Did you know that the oldest tree known to man is approximately four thousand years old? Why? Because the great biblical flood occurred over four thousand years ago. That's no coincidence."

"Hey," says an intrigued Buddy, "are you talking about Noah and the wooden boat?"

"I am indeed," says Hugh. "And for your information, it was called an ark."

Buddy looks at his uncle, wide-eyed in amazement. "You mean it was real?" he asks.

"It most certainly was," Hugh responds. He glances around the table at the others. "Some intellectuals will tell you that science and the Bible are not compatible, but I beg to differ."

"Your 'differing' cost you a teaching position at a very prestigious university," Gertie interjects, looking at her son.

"What happened, Uncle Hugh?" Lulu asks inquisitively.

"Oh, it was just a little disagreement with the dean of the science department."

"Little!" Gertie huffs.

Hugh places his elbow on the table and points his fork at Lulu. "All the evidence points directly to an intelligent creator; there is no denying it. Some of the most brilliant scientific minds in history acknowledge God: Newton, Bacon, and Pasteur, just to name a few."

"I believe in God," a smiling Buddy chimes in.

"And what a brilliant young man you are," Hugh proclaims, winking at his nephew.

"Wasn't Darwin's wife a religious woman?" Warren asks as he pours a glass of lemonade.

"Yes, she was. Can you imagine the turmoil in that household?" Hugh chuckles and reaches for a piece of pie.

Chapter 2

After dinner, everyone convenes to the living room, where the conversation continues late into the evening. Lulu, who is cutting out paper dolls at the kitchen table, glances up when the clock on the mantle begins to toll.

Ding, ding, ding, ding, ding, ding, ding, ding, ding, ding.

"Ten o'clock on the dot," Hugh announces as he looks at his wristwatch.

"All right, my children, I do believe it's time for bed. We've had a long day," says Sybil as she stands to her feet.

"But Mom…" pleads Buddy, in the midst of playing marbles on the floor.

"Don't argue with your mother," Warren intervenes.

"We have church tomorrow," Gertie insists. She gives Buddy a kiss on the head and playfully swats his bottom. "Now off you go."

Lulu and Buddy say their good-nights and then head up the stairs to the bedroom they will share.

"I get the bed by the window," proclaims Buddy, "'cause you had it last time, remember?"

"Oh, all right," Lulu concedes reluctantly.

After washing up, and changing into their pajamas, the two exhausted children climb into their beds and settle in for the night.

"Dad!" Buddy yells down the stairs. "Can you let Jack and Otis in?"

There is a loud bang as the screen door slams shut. Jack and Otis bound up the stairs, into the room, and onto the bed where Buddy is lying.

Warren enters the room as well. "Not on the bed!" he scolds the dogs. The two dogs jump off the bed and lie down on the floor in obedience.

Warren bends down and gives Buddy a kiss on his forehead. "Good night, son."

"You forgot to say good-night to Bongo," Buddy says as he holds a stuffed monkey out in front of him.

"Good night, Bongo," Warren says, patting it on the head.

He then walks over to Lulu and gives her a kiss as well. Lulu wraps her arms around her father's neck and pulls him close to her.

"Are you absolutely, positively positive that there is a God?" she whispers in his ear.

"Beyond the shadow of a doubt positive," he responds, reassuring his daughter.

Relieved, Lulu releases her grip and lets her father go.

"Good night, my children," Warren says as he turns off the light and leaves the room.

Chapter 3

The next morning, Lulu and Buddy are awakened by the smell of breakfast wafting through the air.

"I'll race you downstairs!" Buddy exclaims as he reaches for his glasses on the bedside table.

"Leave me alone!" Lulu snaps as she closes her eyes and pulls the blankets up over her head. Princess, who is curled up next to Lulu, lets out an irritated meow at being disturbed. Buddy, with dogs in tow, rushes down the stairs to the kitchen.

Lulu finally gets up, following much prodding from her mother.

After breakfast, everyone cleans up and then heads outside for the drive to church. Lulu and Buddy climb into the car and sit in the back seat alongside their grandmother. Hugh turns the crank to start the car. He hops in the front seat next to Sybil and Warren, and the car begins to putter down the gravel road.

They pass a farmhouse and a dilapidated barn whose once vibrant red paint has faded to a rusty brown over the years. The cows grazing in the field look up and stare as the car rumbles by. The road ventures to the west, over an old wooden bridge that spans a creek, and then meanders up a small hill and down the other side past the Willis' place. They have a menagerie of coon dogs that howl incessantly when anyone passes by. A rickety sign dangling on the front porch advertises fresh eggs for sale.

Suddenly, a wild turkey dashes across the road in front of them and into the brush. Warren gives the car's horn a squeeze. *"Aah-ooh-gah!"*

"I bet he's the one you couldn't catch," says Lulu with a smirk.

Buddy glares at his sister. "Next time, he won't get away!"

"I'm sure of that," Gertie intercedes, giving Buddy a reassuring pat.

Sometime later, they reach the small, country church nestled in a grove of cedars. The tall, fragrant trees cast a wide shadow, offering relief from the scorching summer sun. Spotting a friend, Buddy is the first one out of the car.

"Henry!" he shouts as he races toward the boy. The two of them then head to the small creek that runs alongside the church.

"Don't get wet!" warns Sybil.

Lulu waits beside her parents as they make small talk with the other parishioners. When the bell begins to toll, they climb the steps and enter the sanctuary where the air is hot and still.

"Oh, how I hate this heat," Sybil murmurs under her breath.

They walk down the aisle and take a seat on one of the long, wooden pews. A few seconds later, Buddy rushes in and sits down next to his father. He is hoping that his mother doesn't notice his wet shoes. She would *not* be happy.

The organist, Mrs. Werner, an elderly woman with gray hair pulled tight into a bun and wire spectacles framing her eyes, takes her place in front of the instrument.

"Please take your hymnals and turn to page 59 as we sing 'Blessed Assurance'," announces Reverend Murphy from the podium. "Let's all stand, shall we?" he asks.

Mrs. Werner plays the introduction and then everyone begins to sing.

Lulu loves to sing, and she is quite good. Daydreaming once again, she is imagining herself on a Parisian stage singing in front of a crowd of enthusiastic admirers. How truly fabulous it would be to travel the world and perform. As much as she fancies this notion, she hasn't decided if she wants to pursue the theater when she grows up, or perhaps be an Egyptologist.

Last year for Christmas, her mother gave her a huge book on the great pyramids and mummies of Egypt. She finds it absolutely fascinating, especially since the recent discovery of King Tutankhamen's tomb.

The thud of her hymnal hitting the wooden floor suddenly brings her back to reality. Embarrassed, Lulu quickly picks up the book.

"You may be seated," Reverend Murphy tells the congregation.

Lulu takes her seat and wipes a bead of sweat from her upper lip. Reverend Murphy begins his sermon, but after ten minutes, Lulu finds it difficult to stay focused. It's hard to pay attention when you are surrounded by a throng of perspiring people in a cramped sanctuary. The ceiling fans whirring overhead offer no relief from the stifling heat.

Buddy starts to fidget in his seat. His wet shoes and socks are making his feet wrinkle like a prune. He looks at his mother and in a loud whisper mutters, "Is it time to go?" She gives him a stern look and presses her index finger to her lips. With a grimace on his face, he crosses his arms, expressing his discontent.

Lulu can feel a trail of perspiration trickle down her back. Bored, she fiddles with the buttons on her dress and glances discreetly around the sanctuary. She spots a handsome, young man several pews up on her right. The woman behind him, however, is wearing a large hat with a feather plume, making it difficult to get a good look.

The minutes slowly tick by, one long second at a time, until Reverend Murphy finally finishes his sermon. Immediately following the closing prayer and the final amen, a multitude of sticky, restless children make a mad dash for the huge double doors at the back of the church.

"I'll try to not take that personal," announces Reverend Murphy with a grin on his face. The adults chuckle at his remark as they slowly file out of the church, chitchatting with one another along the way.

Chapter 4

After the drive home, Lulu helps her mother and grandmother prepare lunch. She heads outside to the garden behind the house, where a scarecrow with a crooked smile and tattered coveralls hangs on a pole. The leaves on the corn stalks, towering over her head, rustle in the breeze. Several black crows, sitting on the wooden fence surrounding the garden, watch Lulu with their dark, beady eyes.

"Shoo, you old birds!" she hollers, waving her hands in the air.

"Caw, caw," the crows squawk in protest and fly away, retreating to the branches of a nearby tree.

Meandering up and down the rows, Lulu picks tomatoes and okra, as well as some fresh strawberries, gently placing them in the fold of her dress, which she is using as a makeshift basket.

Buddy and Hugh, meanwhile, are in the midst of pitching a tent near the woods for a backyard campout. Warren casually thumbs through the latest issue of *Photoplay* magazine as he sits on a step of the back porch.

"Watch your fingers!" he calls out to Buddy, who is helping Hugh drive a stake into the ground.

After lunch, Lulu clears the table and helps her mother wash the dishes. Hugh and Warren head to the living room to listen to the Cardinals baseball game. A small, electric fan hums in the afternoon heat. They huddle in close around the radio, hanging on every word the announcer utters. A few hours later, Sybil enters the room and laughs when she sees the two men asleep, snoring in unison.

"Warren," Sybil says as she nudges her husband, "can you find the children? Dinner will be ready in a bit and they need to wash up."

Awakened from his slumber, Warren rubs his eyes and slowly gets up from the sofa. "Yes, dear," he responds as he heads out the front door and down the porch steps, still groggy from his nap.

"Hang on and I'll go with you," Hugh says as he turns off the radio. He grabs his hat from the hall tree and follows Warren out the door. "I have a feeling I know just where they are."

As the two men make their way down a well-worn dirt path amid tall weeds and overgrown brush, they hear the faint sound of children laughing and dogs barking. They find them just where Hugh thought they'd be: splashing in the water of a natural spring by the mouth of one of the caves that are plentiful in the wooded Ozark Mountains. The crisp, clear water contains a plethora of tadpoles and crawdads. Jack and Otis feverishly dunk their heads in the water, trying to catch the elusive creatures.

"I knew it!" exclaims Hugh. "This used to be my favorite spot on a hot summer day."

"Come on in!" Lulu calls out. "It feels divine."

"Don't mind if I do," Hugh remarks as he takes off his shoes and socks, rolls up the legs of his pants, and plunges his feet into the refreshing water.

Standing on the bank, Warren and Buddy engage in several competitive rounds of rock skipping. Buddy picks up a smooth, flat stone and hurls it across the water's surface. It bounces numerous times before finally sinking to the bottom of the spring.

"That's some arm you've got there, kid!" Hugh exclaims, watching his nephew.

"I've been practicing," Buddy responds proudly, grinning from ear to ear.

Lulu gets out of the water and lies down in the soft, thick grass. The late-afternoon sunlight trickles through the branches of the dense trees surrounding the spring. After picking a handful of purple clover flowers, she ties the ends together, making a circle that she places around her neck.

"We should head back," Hugh suggests glancing at his watch. "We've been gone for over an hour."

As they near the house, they recognize a familiar figure in the distance talking to Gertie and Sybil, who are standing on the front porch.

"It's Peddler Joe!" Buddy points out, as he takes off running.

Peddler Joe has been in these parts for years, going door to door selling various knickknacks and trinkets out of a rickety, old, gypsy wagon pulled by his mule, Penelope. His long gray beard, twinkling blue eyes, and thick German accent have always intrigued Buddy.

"Well, hello there, young man," Peddler Joe announces as Buddy races toward him.

"Got anything good?" Buddy inquires out of breath.

"But of course," says Joe as he rummages through baskets of various items hanging from the wagon. "*Ah-ha.* How 'bout this?" he says holding up an object. "A mighty fine, genuine wooden train whistle."

"Wow!" Buddy exclaims, taking the whistle and giving it a blow.

"Whooh! Whooh!"

"Oh my, that's loud," Gertie winces, clasping her hands over her ears. "Sounds just like a train!"

Lulu and the others gather around the wagon as well.

"And for you, Miss Lulu, how about this lovely charm bracelet?"

Lulu's eyes widen as she takes the bracelet and examines the various charms.

"It's from the 1904 World's Fair held right here in St. Louie!" Peddler Joe exclaims. "I was there, you know," he says, placing a hand on Lulu's shoulder. "It was incredible—the most amazing sights I'd ever seen." A smile spread across his weathered face as he fondly reminisced.

"It's lovely," she responds. "Can you help me put it on?" she asks, turning to her father.

"Oh, I almost forgot," says Peddler Joe as he steps around to the rear of the wagon and reappears with a box. "I stopped by the drugstore when I was in town, and Mr. Sittner asked me to bring this to you." He hands the box to Hugh.

"Finally," says Hugh as he thoroughly inspects the contents.

"What's in there?" Buddy asks inquisitively, trying to peer inside the box.

"Just some things I ordered," Hugh replies.

"Not another experiment, I hope," says Gertie, expressing her concern. "You almost blew up the barn while tinkering on your last gadget," she continues, eyeing her son suspiciously.

"Now Mother, there's no need to exaggerate," he responds.

After paying for the items, Hugh and the others wave good-bye as Peddler Joe and Penelope head down the dusty road in search of their next customer.

"Let's eat before dinner gets cold," Gertie insists as she turns and heads up the porch stairs.

Chapter 5

Following dinner, Sybil and Warren decide to sit a spell on the front porch swing and watch the sun go down. Lulu helps her grandmother put away the dishes, and afterward, the two of them retreat to the sofa to finish knitting the pink scarf and matching hat they've been working on for Lulu to wear this winter.

Buddy and Hugh, who are embattled in a game of checkers, stare at the board in silence. Buddy moves one of his pieces and quickly jumps to his feet in victory.

"I won! You were just beaten by a seven-year-old!" he shouts triumphantly.

"How terribly pathetic," moans Hugh, feigning defeat. He winks at Lulu and gives her a sly grin. Uncle Hugh always lets him win, but Buddy hasn't figured that out yet.

Suddenly, the radio announcer interrupts the musical broadcast that was playing quietly in the background.

> This just in: The legal advisors for Mr. John Scopes will meet tomorrow in New York to discuss the defense strategy for the upcoming trial. Mr. Scopes, a teacher from Dayton, Tennessee, is accused of violating the Butler Act, which prohibits the teaching of evolution. The trial is scheduled to begin on July 10. The proponents of evolution and liberalism will spar against the religious fundamentalists and conservatives in what is being called the 'trial of the century'…

"I never thought I'd see the day," Gertie declares, shaking her head in disbelief. "What has this world come to?"

Hugh stands to his feet and turns off the radio.

"Is anyone up for some stargazing?" he asks as he adjusts the waist of his pants. "The sun will be setting here shortly."

"Me! Me!" shouts Buddy, raising his hand enthusiastically.

"All right then, let's get the old telescope out."

Hugh and Buddy head up the stairs to the attic to retrieve the telescope. At the top of the stairs, Hugh pulls a key from his trousers and unlocks the door to his workshop. Lulu and Buddy have only been in the room on a few select occasions, as their uncle has made it very clear that the room is strictly off-limits.

The old door creaks as it opens, and Buddy enters the room behind his uncle. He glances around to see the contents of the secretive room. A large object, covered in a bed sheet, looms menacingly in the center of the floor.

Curious, Buddy asks, "What's *that,* Uncle Hugh?"

"Oh, just something I'm working on," Hugh replies as he makes his way through the attic.

Buddy lifts the bed sheet, exposing the side of the metallic object.

"Come over here," Hugh says, trying to distract Buddy. "I need your muscles to help me carry this telescope down the stairs."

"Oh, all right," shrugs a disappointed Buddy.

As they leave the room, Buddy takes one more lingering glance at the mysterious contraption, his mind feverishly racing with curious thoughts.

Once downstairs, Hugh sets up the large telescope on the front porch. He looks through the eyepiece and makes several adjustments.

"Coming, Lulu?" he asks through the screen door.

Lulu gets up from the sofa and heads for the porch.

"Buddy, you're up first," Hugh announces.

Buddy eagerly peers through the eyepiece of the telescope and lets out several *oohs* and *aahs* as he stares in amazement at the image he sees.

"My turn," Lulu insists as she nudges Buddy out of the way.

"Hey," Buddy responds in protest, "you big meanie!"

Warren gets up from the porch swing and walks over to the telescope.

"How about giving your ol' dad a peek," he suggests. Warren bends down and takes a look.

"How can anyone say there is no God?" Hugh asks as he places his hands on his hips and stares at the beautiful night sky. "Just look at the heavens so full of wonder and awe. This is not the result of some random explosion. Oh no! This," he proclaims, opening his arms wide, "was thoughtfully designed by a brilliant creator with absolute precision and order."

"It's quite spectacular," Buddy interjects.

"My, what a big word for such a small boy," chuckles Gertie, who is watching from behind the screen door. "Did you learn that in school?" she asks.

"Yep," he responds proudly.

For the next two hours, everyone takes turns looking at the cosmos through the large telescope as Hugh points out the various constellations. Soon, however, their view is obscured by the arrival of dense, dark-gray clouds.

"Uh oh, those are cumulonimbus clouds," Hugh states, eyeing the horizon. "That means a thunderstorm is rolling in. We better batten down the hatches; it could be a doozey."

The winds start to pick up and everyone heads inside before the rain and hail arrive.

"Does that mean no campout?" Buddy asks with obvious disappointment in his voice.

"I'm afraid not," Hugh replies. "We'll do it another day."

Hugh and Buddy return the telescope to the attic. Using the key in his pocket, Hugh locks the door securely behind him. "Oh my, I didn't realize it was so late," he says, glancing at his watch. "I think it's time for you to go to bed, mister."

"But I'm not tired," Buddy moans in protest.

"Come on," says Hugh as he takes Buddy by the hand. "We've got all week for adventure."

Chapter 6

Sybil and Warren tuck their children into bed and kiss them good-night. Buddy, holding Bongo tightly, peers out the window as the rain trickles down the glass.

"Dad…"

"Yes, son."

"Tell me about Noah."

Warren sits down on the side of the bed next to him. "What do you want to know?" Warren asks, tousling Buddy's hair.

"Like what happened, and why. I mean, why would God flood the earth?" Buddy asks, clearly troubled at the thought.

"Well, during Noah's time, the people were very wicked. They turned away from God and did bad things."

Buddy looks at his father. "Like what?"

"All kinds of things, I suppose. I'm sure it must have been pretty awful for God to be so angry."

"Why did God save Noah?" Buddy asks.

"Noah loved God, but the others forgot about Him and did whatever they wanted, and that made God very sad. He regretted ever making them and decided to destroy them all, except for Noah and his family. So God told Noah to build a—"

"Ark!" Buddy interjects.

"Yes, an ark," Warren confirms. "God told him exactly how to build it—how long, how tall, how wide, and even the type of wood to use. When the ark was finished, God told Noah to put every kind of animal in it."

"I wish he would have left out spiders and snakes!" Lulu quips from her bed, wrinkling her nose in obvious disgust.

Warren laughs at his daughter's remark and continues. "So Noah did as God said, and he and his family entered the ark and the door was closed behind them. And then the rain began to fall."

Suddenly, a bolt of lightning flashes outside the window, followed by a loud clap of thunder. Startled, Buddy pulls the blankets up under his chin.

"Do you really think that happened?" asks Lulu, who is propped up on her elbow. "Some of the kids at school say the Bible is just a book of made-up fairy tales."

"I suppose it may sound a bit far-fetched," Warren responds. "But I believe it."

He stands to his feet. "All right now, you two, it's way past your bedtime. We can talk more about this tomorrow."

Buddy takes his train whistle off the nightstand and gives it a blow.

"Whooh! Whooh!"

"Not now, son." Warren says taking the whistle from Buddy and slipping it into the pocket of his pants. He kisses Lulu and Buddy good-night, turns off the light, and closes the door behind him.

Chapter 7

Throughout the night, the rain continues to beat down on the old house, pinging loudly off the tin roof. Buddy gets up out of his bed and in the darkness makes his way over to Lulu, who is sound asleep.

"Lulu, Lulu," he whispers as he gently nudges his sister. "I can't sleep."

"Go back to bed and close your eyes!" she snaps.

"I tried that, but they keep opening," he responds in frustration.

Suddenly, they hear a loud thud in the attic, followed by incoherent mumbling.

Lulu quickly sits up in her bed. "What was *that*?" she asks.

"I bet it's Uncle Hugh in his workshop," says Buddy. "He's probably working on his secret invention."

"What are you talking about?" Lulu asks curiously.

"Come on," replies Buddy. "Follow me."

The two children quietly sneak up the attic stairs and peer under the door. They watch in amazement as their uncle frantically works on the odd contraption.

"What *is* it?" Lulu asks in a hushed whisper.

"I don't know," Buddy responds. "Uncle Hugh wouldn't tell me." He thinks for a moment and then mutters nervously, "What if he's making a monster?" His brown eyes were wide with fear and intrigue at the thought.

"There's no such thing as monsters, silly," Lulu replies, trying to reassure her little brother.

They continue watching their uncle from the crack beneath the door. Hugh looks around the room. He spies an old, clay, garden gnome in the corner of the attic. "Do you like to travel, old guy?" he asks as he picks up the sun-faded figurine and places it in the middle of a chalk circle drawn on the floor. "I hope so, because you're about to take a trip."

Hugh puts on a pair of aviator goggles, stands behind the machine, and manipulates several different levers and knobs. With a blinding flash of light, the gnome suddenly disappears.

"It worked!" announces Hugh, trying desperately to contain his excitement. "I actually did it. Wait until the world hears about this!"

Unbeknownst to anyone, Hugh has opened a portal that is able to transport people and objects through time. Still in awe of what just happened, Hugh removes the goggles, sits down at his desk, and begins to write frantically in his journal.

He continues writing and mumbling for quite some time, until every last detail of his experiment is noted.

Once complete, he closes the journal and turns off the desk lamp.

Exhausted, Hugh stands up, stretches his arms over his head, and lets out a sigh, ready to turn in for the night.

"Not just handsome but brilliant as well," he says as he gives himself a pat on the chest and heads for the door.

Lulu and Buddy scurry down the stairs to their room before he sees them.

After a few minutes, Buddy opens the door and gazes down the narrow hallway. "He's gone, and I don't think he locked the door," he announces with a mischievous grin on his face. "Let's go have a look."

"No, Buddy, we're not supposed to go in there!"

"Oh come on, you big scaredy-cat!" Buddy taunts.

Buddy quietly creeps up the stairs, opens the door, and sneaks into the attic. Jack and Otis follow their master into the mysterious room.

"You shouldn't be in there," says Lulu as she peers cautiously into the room.

Buddy pulls the sheet off the machine and it drops to the floor. "Wow," says Buddy, pushing buttons and turning knobs. "This is neat."

"Don't touch it!" Lulu exclaims as she lunges forward.

There is a huge flash of light followed by eerie silence.

Chapter 8

The next morning, with the rain continuing to pour outside, Hugh heads back up the attic stairs, eager to get back to his workshop. He reaches for the key in his pocket when he notices that the door is slightly ajar.

"I can't believe I forgot to lock it," he says to himself.

He pushes the door open and sees Jack and Otis lying next to the time machine. "What in the world are you two doing in here? Go on now, get out of here," he says as he tries to shoo the whimpering dogs downstairs. Jack and Otis, however, do not budge.

Hugh suddenly realizes the gravity of the situation. He scrambles down the stairs, flinging open the door to the children's room.

"Lulu! Buddy!" he frantically calls out.

Hugh glances around the room, but they are nowhere to be found.

"Oh no!" he wails.

"What is going on?" demands Warren, standing in the doorway and rubbing his eyes.

"I'm afraid the children are in danger!" exclaims Hugh as he tries to catch his breath.

"What are you talking about?" asks Sybil, who is now standing behind Warren, tying the belt of her robe.

"Please… just come with me," Hugh pleads.

They rush to the attic and are soon joined by Gertie.

"What in heaven's name is *that?*" she asks pointing to the machine.

"I've devised a time transporter, a portal of sorts, and I think Lulu and Buddy have opened it."

"Are you saying they're… gone?" Warren asks, confused.

"Yes," Hugh responds, "I'm afraid so."

Sybil gasps and puts her hand over her mouth. Gertie, suddenly feeling faint, slumps down in a chair.

"But, but… how?" Warren stammers, trying to make sense of the situation.

"It has to do with negative energy, and…"

"What?" asks a perplexed Warren.

"I don't have time to explain," says an exasperated Hugh. "We have to go after them!"

Hugh grabs the journal off his desk and hands it to his sister.

"Sybil, you must do exactly as I've written."

"But Hugh…"

Hugh grabs her by the shoulders and shakes her.

"Listen to me. It's up to you to open and close the portal."

"I can't!" exclaims a terrified Sybil.

"You *don't* have a choice," he says sternly as he looks her in the eye.

Hugh grabs a watch from his desk. Frantically, he winds the timepiece and compares it to the watch on his wrist.

"They must be perfectly synchronized. Tomorrow morning, precisely at 9:00, turn on the machine to open the portal. Leave it on for ten minutes, and then turn it off. Do this every day until we return, for as long as it takes! Do you understand?" Hugh thrusts the watch into Sybil's trembling hand.

Sybil is silent.

"Sybil, you've got to do it. This is our only hope."

Reluctantly, she nods her head and begins to sob.

"We must leave now!" says Hugh as he turns to face Warren.

"Oh, dear God!" Gertie wails.

"I'm not even dressed," says Warren, realizing he is still in his pajamas.

"Hurry!" yells a frantic Hugh. "We've no time to waste!"

Warren rushes down the stairs and returns a moment later, scrambling to button his shirt as he enters the room. Sybil embraces him and buries her face in his chest.

"I love you, dear," she says in-between sobs. He wraps his arms around her and kisses her forehead.

Hugh picks up a knapsack and feverishly dumps its contents on the floor. After rummaging through the desk drawer, he puts a pocketknife, rope, compass, and several other items into the bag.

"Where are we going?" Warren asks, filled with concern.

"I'm not sure," Hugh responds, unable to hide the fear and uncertainty in his voice. He approaches the machine and starts frantically turning the knobs.

"All right, Warren, it's time."

Warren embraces Sybil one last time and whispers in her ear, "Pray, Sybil. Pray like you've never prayed before."

Warren then takes his place next to Hugh in the middle of the chalk circle.

"Pull the lever, Sybil!" Hugh shouts.

Hesitantly, she approaches the machine.

"Now!" yells Hugh.

Sybil holds her breath as she pulls the lever. Instantly, Hugh and Warren are gone. She wonders if she will ever see her husband, brother, or children again.

Chapter 9

Transported through time to an unknown location, Hugh and Warren arrive in the midst of a fierce, driving rain. Unsure of where they are, the two men desperately survey their surroundings, trying to get their bearings.

Nothing looks familiar. Gone is the lush, green landscape of the Missouri countryside. In its place is a vast expanse of barren land and desert, which is quickly becoming a muddy sandpit in the unrelenting rain.

After a few moments of scanning the terrain, Warren spots something glistening in the mud. He bends down and picks up the object. As he wipes away the dirt, he immediately recognizes the item: a charm from Lulu's bracelet.

"They're here!" shouts a relieved Warren.

Hugh then notices small, obscure footprints barely visible in the mud. "Thank God!" he exclaims. Glancing around, he spies the garden gnome half-buried in the mud and pulls it free.

"What is that?" Warren asks with obvious confusion.

"I'll explain later," Hugh responds.

Immediately, he starts to gather large rocks, stacking them in a pile on top of one another. "We must mark this location so we know our point of entry. It's imperative that we return to this exact spot in order to return through the portal," he asserts as he continues erecting the formation.

Warren joins in the task. After stacking the rocks several feet high and wide, Hugh tears a sleeve from his shirt and ties it around the head of the gnome. He then places the figurine on top of the stone structure.

"That should do it," says Hugh as he wipes his rain-soaked face. He checks the compass and attempts to plot their location. After making note of it, he picks up the knapsack and grabs Warren by the arm. "Come on. We've got to follow the footprints before they're washed away."

The rain continues to beat down as they make their way across the soggy terrain. Cold and shivering, the two men press on, determined to find Lulu and Buddy.

After struggling up a hill, they finally reach its crest and vaguely make out a large village in the distance. It is still miles away.

"Let's head there," Hugh suggests.

Weary, they continue on their trek.

Chapter 10

Sometime later, as Hugh and Warren finally near the town, they hear a disturbing commotion going on. People are hysterical—shouting and crying—but the men cannot make out what they are saying. It is not a language they are familiar with. The place seems to be some sort of large Bedouin settlement or trading center. It is obvious that Hugh and Warren are foreigners, but in the midst of the hysteria, no one seems to notice the two strangers.

Despite the odd circumstances, Warren's only concern is his children. "They've got to be here," he says, running through the muddy streets, pushing past people and frantically looking in the crudely made buildings.

"Lulu! Buddy!" he shouts.

With Hugh following close behind, they make their way through a maze of narrow alleyways that wind through the village. For several hours, they continue searching in the merciless rain, desperate to find the two lost children. All the buildings seem to look alike, adding to their frustration.

Exhausted, Warren slips in the mud and collapses on the ground. The frenzied crowd nearly tramples him, but Hugh drags him to a nearby doorway, out of harm's way. Hugh then falls on his knees beside Warren. Emotionally and physically drained, they struggle to catch their breath. Warren opens his mouth and tilts his head back, trying to quench his parched throat with the falling rain.

"We mustn't give up," Hugh stammers.

Warren hangs his head and whispers a prayer, hoping to thwart the overwhelming despair washing over him. With his face covered in mud, he reaches into his pants pocket to retrieve a handkerchief. As he pulls it out, something falls to the ground. Warren and Hugh look at the object. It's Buddy's train whistle. Warren grabs it.

"If they're here, they'll recognize the sound," he announces with renewed hope. Without hesitation, they clamber to their feet and continue on their search.

The two men weave and bob their way through the horde of people as Warren frantically blows the whistle. *"Whooh! Whooh! Whooh! Whooh!"*

"The sun is beginning to set," Warren observes in frustration. "We've got to find them."

"We'll have a better view from up there," Hugh says, pointing to the roof of a building.

Hugh helps Warren scramble up the side of the mud structure and onto the roof. Warren continues to blow the whistle as he runs across the rooftop, scanning the crowd below.

Chapter 11

Not far away, Buddy, terrified and cold, glances up from the dark corner he and Lulu are huddled in.

"My whistle," he announces. "It sounds like my whistle."

"Are you sure?" Lulu asks hesitantly, not wanting to leave the safety of the refuge they have found.

"Yes!" he replies.

Emerging from their hiding place, the two children try to discern the direction the sound is coming from. Hand in hand, they attempt to make their way through the frenzied crowd. Suddenly, Lulu spots her father on a nearby roof.

"Up there. It's Dad!"

The two children jump up and down, screaming and waving as they desperately try to get the attention of their father. However, the crowd around them is so loud that Warren is unable to hear their cries.

Buddy bends down and grabs a pebble from the ground, then hurls it toward his father. He misses but tries again. This time, it lands a few feet from Warren on the rooftop.

Startled, Warren picks up the rock and looks around to see where it came from. He scans the crowd below, looking for the familiar faces of his children.

"I see them!" Warren motions to Hugh. "Over there, over there!" he yells, pointing to Lulu and Buddy.

Hugh pushes through the mob of villagers until he reaches them.

"Uncle Hugh!" shouts Buddy, rushing into his uncle's arms.

Warren shimmies down from the roof and makes his way to where they are.

"Dad," Lulu says in-between sobs, "I knew you'd come."

Warren embraces his children. "Oh, thank God," he gasps, barely able to contain his emotion. "Are you all right?" he asks as he looks them over.

They are barefoot, in their pajamas, and soaked head to toe from the unrelenting rain.

"I'm scared and I want to go home," says Lulu as she holds her father tightly.

"Dad," Buddy stammers, his teeth chattering from the cold, "there are giants here!"

"Giants?" Warren asks in disbelief.

"They're huge and scary," Buddy continues, "and they have six fingers on each hand."

Warren looks at Hugh with concern. "Where exactly are we?" he asks.

"I don't know," Hugh says, puzzled by the situation. "It's utter and complete pandemonium here."

He grabs a young man by the shoulders and desperately tries to communicate. "What's happening?" he asks.

Terrified, the young man frantically points to something in the distance and shouts unintelligible words they do not understand.

"What could it be?" Warren wonders.

Hugh looks at his brother-in-law. "There's only one way to find out."

Chapter 12

They make their way to the edge of the village, and once there, push their way through a tide of people, standing shoulder to shoulder, trying to see for themselves the cause of such great chaos.

"I can't believe it," mutters a stunned Hugh as he stares at a massive object looming in the valley below.

"What is it, Uncle Hugh?" asks Buddy, standing on his tippy toes, trying to get a glimpse.

"It looks like the—"

"Ark," interjects Warren in a barely audible voice, his gaze fixed on the large wooden vessel.

The ark? Like Noah's ark?" Buddy asks, his eyes growing wide in dismay.

"But Uncle Hugh, if that's the ark, then this must be the… the flood," stammers Lulu as she shivers in the rain.

"Now it all makes sense," Hugh explains as he rubs his head. "Before the flood, it had never rained. There were subterranean springs that watered the earth's vegetation. These people have never seen rain."

"What about the giants?" Buddy asks nervously.

"Nephilim—the Bible mentions a race of people who were the descendants of fallen angels."

"Are they good or bad?" Buddy asks.

"Bad, I'm afraid. Very bad," Hugh responds.

Frightened, Lulu grabs her father's hand. "Please, Dad, let's go home," she begs as tears roll down her cheeks.

In disbelief, Hugh shakes his head. "I can't believe I actually did it," he mutters under his breath.

"What do you mean?" asks Warren, still in shock.

Hugh turns to face Warren. "I wanted to prove the existence of God, so I created the time machine."

Stunned, Warren responds, "So this wasn't an accident? You did this on purpose?" he says, raising his voice in anger.

"My plan was to travel to a significant historical event in the Bible and return with some sort of proof that it occurred. Something that would convince the world that God *does* exist."

"The *flood*, of all things, you had to pick the *flood*? What were you thinking?"

"Unfortunately, my calculations were a bit off, I'm afraid," Hugh admits. "I never meant for you or the children to be a part of this."

"But we *are*!" an infuriated Warren shouts, desperately trying to process what he's been told.

Aware of the dire situation, they stand in silence despite the hysterical crowd around them.

"We've got to get out of here," Warren insists. "Obviously, this rain is not going to stop."

"Just let me document this," Hugh says as he rummages through his knapsack. "A few photos, that's all I need!" he exclaims as he removes a camera from his bag. "This could end the debate once and for all." Feverishly, he begins to snap photos of the ark and the incredible scene playing out before their very eyes.

"What good are pictures if we don't make it back?" Warren asks in frustration.

Without warning, the ground beneath them begins to rumble violently.

"Run!" Hugh shouts as he grabs Lulu and Buddy by the arm and makes a mad dash for safety. Suddenly, a huge explosion of water bursts forth from the earth, spewing high into the air.

"The underground water reservoirs are erupting. We've got to make our way back! Things are going to get really bad really fast." Hugh pulls the compass from his knapsack. "According to my notes, the portal is about fifteen miles due east of here," he says, eyeing the horizon. "It could take all night," he continues, aware of the difficult journey that lies ahead.

Chapter 13

Night falls and dark, gray clouds cover the moon as the relentless rain continues to beat down, pelting them as they slowly trudge through the murky water. Geysers burst forth across the landscape and screams of terror echo in the distance. Violent earthquakes shake the ground beneath their feet.

Warren and Hugh carry the exhausted children in their arms as they navigate through the swirling torrent of water, which is now waist deep. A bitterly cold wind, howling around them, adds to their difficult situation.

As day breaks, the sun's rays are unable to pierce the thick clouds that hover overhead.

"I think we are being followed," Warren announces.

Hugh turns around to see for himself. Looming in the distance are several large, menacing figures quickly making their way through the water toward them.

"That looks like the giant I saw," Buddy says nervously.

Glancing over his shoulder, Warren watches as the giants follow, quickly gaining ground on them.

Warren grabs Hugh by the arm. "Why are they following us?" he asks, baffled by the situation.

"They know we aren't from here."

"What do they want?"

Hugh looks at Warren and in a quivering voice responds, "Us."

Chapter 14

Back at the farmhouse, Gertie and Sybil anxiously wait. Gripping the timepiece tightly in one hand and Hugh's instructions in the other, Sybil paces back and forth as the old wooden floor creaks noisily beneath her.

"What time is it?" Gertie asks as she nervously wrings her hands.

Sybil pauses to look at the watch. "Eight twenty-seven," she responds.

The pounding rain continues to pour outside as ominous storm clouds hover over the house. Several bolts of lightning flash across the morning sky. Gertie crosses the room and peers out the window. A torrent of water beats against the glass. "I've never seen it rain like this before," she observes, her eyes darting across the horizon. "There's something very odd about it."

The wind begins to blow, howling ferociously. Another bolt of lightning dances across the dark-purple sky as the two women stare out the window, their silhouettes barely casting a shadow in the dimly lit room.

Gertie glances at the watch in Sybil's hand. Once again, they begin to pace the floor as the last remaining minutes slowly tick away. Finally, Sybil turns to Gertie and announces, "It's time." She quickly makes her way to the machine and flips the main switch.

She wipes her brow and stammers as she reads from Hugh's journal, careful to follow his instructions exactly as they are written.

After making the final adjustment, she takes a step back, nervously watching for any sign of life from the machine. She pushes aside a wisp of blonde hair that has fallen in front of her eyes, holds her breath, and waits. Haltingly, the lights on the control panel begin to illuminate, and the large metal contraption starts to rumble.

The portal slowly opens, and a cold, gray mist appears, swirling around Sybil and Gertie, quickly enveloping the room. Rain, pouring in from the portal, pelts the attic floor.

"What in the world is going on?" Gertie asks.

"Warren! Hugh!" Sybil yells into the dark hole. "Are you there?"

There is no response.

Using the sleeve of her dress, Sybil wipes the rain from her face. She looks at the watch. It's six minutes after nine. She peers into the vortex, unable to see anything other than darkness. Stretching out her arms, she reaches into the black void, encountering a cold she has never felt before—a bitter cold that bores into her bones.

"Be careful, Sybil!" her mother calls out.

Without warning, an enormous clap of thunder shakes the house to its foundation.

"Boom!"

The attic windows rattle and the floorboards heave tossing the women like ragdolls to their knees.

The ceiling light flickers eerily overhead, and then goes out completely.

Sybil scrambles to her feet and rushes to the time machine, only to see that its lights have gone off as well.

"No, no, no, this can't be happening!" she screams as she pounds her fist on the large metal object.

The machine is silent.

Chapter 15

Hugh and the others rush to reach the portal entry as the giants close in on them. "It's six minutes after nine," he shouts, standing on top of the stone structure. "It should be open!"

The hair on the back of Hugh's neck stands up on end as an unearthly, guttural growl pierces the air. He makes eye contact with one of the giants, sending a surge of fear through his body.

"Dad, I'm afraid," Lulu whimpers as she stands next to her father, gripping his arm.

"Do something!" Warren yells while looking at Hugh. He grabs a stick floating in the water and swings it, trying to fend off the sinister creatures.

Long, matted hair hangs over their grotesque and misshapen faces, and their eyes are dark like bottomless pits. Lulu and Buddy scream in terror as the giants form a circle around them. The rocks give way under the children, causing Lulu to fall into the water. Buddy quickly grabs his sister, pulling her to safety.

"God, help us!" Hugh shouts in desperation.

A bolt of lightning zigzags across the sky and a strange wind begins to blow. The portal opens, revealing a black void.

"Lulu, Buddy, go! Go!" Warren screams as he shoves the children through the portal.

Lulu and Buddy disappear from view just as one of the giants lunges for Hugh.

"Save yourself!" he tells Warren.

"No!" Warren screams. "I'm not leaving without you!"

As Warren starts to blur and disappear, he thrusts his hand out to Hugh. One of the giants grabs the knapsack on Hugh's back and a vicious tug of war ensues. Just as Warren starts to lose his grip on Hugh, the strap on the knapsack breaks, and all of its contents, including the camera, fall into the water.

"My camera!" Hugh shouts as the bag quickly fades from sight in the dark swirling current.

"Let it go!" Warren screams. "It's not worth it!"

Hugh turns around and the two men disappear into the dark hole.

Chapter 16

In the attic of the farmhouse, the light flickers overhead, and the machine rumbles back to life. The two women scramble to their feet as the portal opens and rain begins to pour in at an alarming rate. A fierce wind whips around the room, flinging items in the air and knocking the women back to the ground.

"Get under the desk!" Sybil shouts to her mother, who is desperately crawling across the floor on her hands and knees.

Sybil manages to stand to her feet and approaches the portal.

"Lulu! Buddy!" she screams. "Is anybody there?"

A window shatters when a flying object slams against the frame, spewing shards of glass around the room.

A hand slowly emerges from the darkness of the portal.

"It's Buddy!" Sybil says as she grabs hold and pulls her son to safety. Lulu quickly follows, but Warren and Hugh are still missing.

After several tense moments, Warren and Hugh finally stumble out of the portal and collapse, out of breath, onto the floor.

"They're coming!" Hugh gasps. "Turn it off! Turn it off!"

Sybil frantically pulls the plug from the wall. A horrendous shriek emanates from within the black portal, which closes and disappears before their very eyes.

The wind and rain abruptly cease, the gray clouds part and the sun breaks through the darkness. They watch in amazement as a brilliant rainbow arches majestically across the sky.

Chapter 17

Gertie puts a pot of coffee on the stove as the others sit quietly around the table, numb and exhausted from the harrowing journey. The repetitive tick-tock of the mantle clock is the only sound in the room.

"I'm sorry for everything," Hugh begins, breaking the silence. "I never meant for this to happen," he continues with a solemn expression on his face.

"Well, I'm just thankful everyone is home safe and sound," Gertie says as she places a cup on the table. "You gave us all quite a scare."

"Mom, you should have seen the ark," Buddy says, turning to Sybil. "It was huge!"

"You really saw it?" she asks in disbelief as she places her arm around his shoulder and pulls him close.

"We really did," Warren interjects as he sips his coffee. "And to think that Noah was actually there—on the ark. It's mind-boggling."

"Uncle Hugh took pictures," Buddy says, glancing up at his mother. "We're going to be famous!" he exclaims as he adjusts his glasses and takes a bite of toast. "Just wait 'til the kids at school hear about this."

Hugh fidgets with a spoon on the table and exchanges a look with Warren before reluctantly turning to his nephew to break the news. "I dropped the camera, Buddy. The pictures are gone."

"You… you did?" Buddy stammers in surprise. "But what are we going to show the people? How will they know it really happened?"

"It was a foolish idea to begin with, and we mustn't tell anyone," Hugh says as he drops the spoon and looks around the table at the others.

"Not even Mr. Peabody?" Lulu asks.

"Definitely not Mr. Peabody," Warren warns his daughter.

"We still have the time machine," Buddy adds hopefully. "We could show them that."

"No, Buddy, you don't understand," Hugh responds. "If it got into the wrong hands, the results could be catastrophic." He stands to his feet and paces across the kitchen floor, trying to process his thoughts. He pauses a moment before slamming his fist on the table, startling the others. "It's just too dangerous. I've got to destroy it!"

"No," Buddy pleads as tears stream down his face. "You can't. Please, Uncle Hugh."

Sybil gently pats her son on the back, trying to comfort him.

"Buddy, I'm sorry..." Hugh trails off in frustration. "There will always be people who don't believe in God. That's just the way it is."

"You can prove it, Uncle Hugh," Lulu interjects. "Isn't that why you built the time machine in the first place?"

Hugh shakes his head. "God doesn't need my help. The evidence is there; some just choose not to see it."

"But…"

"Now, now dear," Gertie says, placing a hand on Lulu's shoulder. "Faith means believing with your heart and not with your eyes." She pauses as her voice quivers with emotion. "Regardless of what the world may say, we must never doubt that there is a God."

Lulu nods her head.

"God *is* real, and He loves us very much," Gertie adds as she dabs her eyes with the hem of her apron. She clears her throat and heads to the sink to compose herself.

Once again, the room falls silent. Hugh excuses himself and retreats to the attic while the others continue to sit around the table.

After much contemplation, Hugh reluctantly decides not to destroy the time machine but to dismantle it instead. Piece by piece, he takes it apart and places it in wooden crates that are moved to a dark, recessed corner of the barn. He throws a tattered, wool blanket over the heap and heads for the door.

As he exits the barn, he squints and shields his eyes from the bright midday sun. From inside the house Buddy peers through the window, his forehead pressed against the glass. He watches as Hugh closes the large wooden door and locks it securely, putting the key in his pocket.

Afterword

I thoroughly enjoyed this wonderful adventure story about learning to trust God. The great lie today is that you can either be smart or believe in God, but not both. This is not true! Great scientists of the past, like Isaac Newton, believed in God. I am a scientist too, and I believe in God!

The Christian faith is not simply a blind faith. It is a faith proven by history, natural science, psychology, medicine, sociology, and every field of knowledge. These different areas of knowledge are "bread crumbs" left by God in order that we might discover Him and His great love for us. It is an exciting journey of discovery!

Mel Campbell, Adjunct Physics Professor
California Baptist University

What an exciting story, leaves you wanting more. There is more! The Bible is God's Word, and it tells us the story of creation, mankind's fall into sin, and the arrival of Jesus, God's son, who came to the world to save us. Think about that!

In order to understand the message, you must start at the beginning. The book of Genesis means "beginnings". In the beginning, God created the heavens and the earth. All things came into being by Him. God not only created the world, He created you. He has a good plan and purpose for your life. Place your faith in Him. Trust Him for your salvation. He will see you through the good times and bad times and guide you safely home.

Michael Lantz, Senior Pastor
Living Truth Christian Fellowship
www.livingtruthcorona.org

For Questions & Answers Visit:

www.AlwaysBeReady.com

Made in the USA
Columbia, SC
03 June 2020